Billy, Tidy Up Your Toys!

By Pamela Malcolm

Aryla Publishing

For my wonderful children, nieces and nephews and to keeping toys tidy ☺.

Please also visit my author page to get more books in the Billy series & Ruby series.

Billy Series
Billy Go To Bed
Billy Get Ready For School
Billy Brush Your Teeth
Billy Eat Your Veg
Billy Tidy Up Your Toys
Billy's Halloween
Billy's Fireworks Night
Billy's Christmas
Billy's Day Out In London
Billy's Easter Egg Hunt
Billy Goes Ice Skating
Billy Goes Swimming
Billy Series Bundle Books 1-5
Billy Goes To Spain

Ruby Series
Ruby Won't Use Her Potty
Ruby's New Shoes
Ruby's Christmas
Ruby No More Binky (Dummy)

Emergency Services Series
Fiona Fire Engine
Percy Police Car

Billy loved to play. He had crayons and cranes, tractors and trains, robots and racing cars, dinosaurs and dominoes, building blocks and boats. He had hula hoops and baseballs. He had spinning tops and marbles. He had water guns and footballs and rubber ducks and a teddy bear called Scuffles - he really liked Scuffles. He had lots and LOTS of toys.

Billy played in his bedroom. He played in the kitchen. He played in the back yard. He played in the hall. He played EVERYWHERE…

but he never, ever tidied up his toys.

"Put your toys back in the toy box," Mum said, "and tidy your room please."

"I can't," said Billy. "I might get too tired and I will not be able to go to school."

"That's a bit silly, Billy," said Mum.

Then Dad said "put your toys back in the toy box and tidy your room please."

"I can't," said Billy. "Scuffles likes it in the kitchen. If I put the toys away, he will have nothing to play with!"

"That's a bit silly, Billy," said Dad.

Grandpa said "put your toys back in the toy box and tidy your room please. Someone might trip over your toys and get hurt."

"There is a very, VERY good reason why I must not tidy my room," said Billy.

"What is that?" Grandpa asked.

All the toys will fight each other in the toy box,"
Billy answered. "They will keep me awake!"
"That's a bit silly, Billy," said Grandpa.
Mum, Dad and Grandpa were worried. All little
boys should tidy their rooms. How else can they
keep the house safe for everyone?
After dinner Dad took Billy upstairs.
Billy had a bath.
He put on his pyjamas.
He brushed his teeth.
He kissed Mum, and Grandpa then Dad tucked
him up in bed and read him a bedtime story.

When Dad was finished, he kissed Billy.

"Goodnight Billy," he said.

"Goodnight Dad," said Billy.

Soon, Billy was fast asleep. In his dreams, Billy flew to the planet Zobloo and met his alien friends: Floo, Choo and Sloo.

"We are glad you are here, Billy," said Floo. "We have a big problem."

"Baby Moo has lost her teddy bear," said Choo. "We are looking for it, but we cannot find it!"

"She will not go to sleep without her teddy bear," said Sloo.

"She is very upset," they all said.

"I have a teddy bear called Scuffles" said Billy. "I will give her Scuffles. Just until you find hers. I really like Scuffles."

"Hooray!" said Floo, Choo and Sloo.

The next morning, Billy looked in his toy box for Scuffles…

but Scuffles was nowhere to be found.

"Mum!" he called. "Where is Scuffles?"

"I don't know, Billy" said Mum. "You were playing with him yesterday."

"But Baby Moo needs him!" said Billy.

"I know how to find Scuffles," said Grandpa. "but it will be hard work, Billy."

"I will work hard!" said Billy. "I really, really, REALLY have to find Scuffles!"

"Well," said Grandpa, "if you pick up all your toys, one by one, and put them back in your toy box, you are sure to find Scuffles."

So that is what Billy did. It was hard work. He did not like it, but he found his teddy bear. Scuffles was the very last toy he picked up. Billy was very happy.

"You are very, VERY good at tidying up, Billy," said Grandpa. Billy was delighted.

That night, Billy showed Scuffles to Floo, Choo and Sloo.

"Hooray!" said Floo.

"Now Baby Moo can go to sleep," said Choo.

"She has missed her teddy bear *so* much," said Sloo.

"Thank you, Billy!" they all said.

Baby Moo was in her cradle. Billy gave her Scuffles. Baby Moo took Scuffles and cuddled him. Soon she was fast asleep.

"Hooray!" said Floo.

"Shhhh!" whispered Choo, Sloo and Billy.

"Now," said Billy, *very* quietly, "we have to find her teddy."

"Her toys are everywhere!" said Floo.

"We will have to tidy up," said Choo.

"It's such a big job!" said Sloo.

"Do not worry," said Billy. "I am very, VERY good at tidying up."

Billy and the aliens picked up all Baby Moo's toys and put them in her toy box.

Baby Moo's teddy bear was the very last toy they picked up.

Billy took Scuffles from her arms, and gave her back her own teddy bear instead. She squeezed it tight, but she stayed fast asleep. When the rest of the aliens in Zobloo found out what Billy had done, they all shouted "hooray for Billy!" Billy was very pleased with himself. They gave him a big gold medal. They put on a big parade for him, and all the aliens cheered for him.

"Thank you, Billy," said Floo, Choo and Sloo.

"It must have been very hard for you to give up Scuffles," said Floo.

"Even if it was only for a little while," said Choo.

"You are very brave, Billy!" said Sloo.

"The next time Baby Moo needs her teddy," said Floo.

We will ask for you," said Choo.

"Because you are very good at tidying up," said Sloo.

"You should put her toys back in her toy box as soon as she is done playing with them," Billy told them. "Someone could trip on then, and get hurt! If you tidy up the toys you will always know where they are."

"We will remember that," the aliens said. "You are so smart, thank you Billy!"

The next day, Billy told Mum, Dad and Grandpa how he had helped Baby Moo to sleep, and how he had found her teddy bear.

"I knew what to do, because I always pick up my toys, you see," he said proudly.

Mum, Dad and Grandpa laughed and said, "you silly Billy!"

After that, Billy played with Scuffles all day.

Just before bedtime, Mum said to Billy, "put your toys back in the toy box, and tidy your room, please."

"There is a very, VERY good reason why I must not tidy my room," said Billy.

"What is that?" Mum, Dad and Grandpa asked.

"Well I am going to play with them tomorrow," Billy said. "So, there is no point putting them away now."

"Oh, Billy!" said Mum, Dad and Grandpa.

But Billy was only teasing. He put away all his toys.

Every last one.

THE END

Thank you for reading……..

Please remember to leave a review if you enjoyed my book it would be nice to hear what you and your children thought of this book☺

Thank you for your time.

Pamel

If you enjoyed this book please also check out these books in the Billy, Ruby and Emergency Services Series below.......

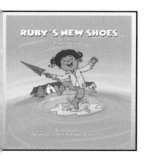
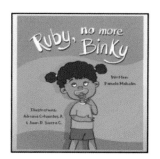

Check out **Billy's Vlogs Monthly** on **YouTube** to find out what he has been up to.

Please visit **www.arylapublishing.com** for more books by **Pamela Malcolm** and other great Authors. Sign up to be informed of upcoming free book promotions and a chance to win prizes in our monthly prize draw.

You can also follow us on **Facebook Instagram & Twitter**

Thank you for your support!

Printed in Great Britain
by Amazon